Judy Brook

HECTOR & HARRIET
THE NIGHT HAMSTERS
Two Adventures

For Maz, Maria and Lalli
in memory of Smee

Copyright © 1984 by Judy Brook
All rights reserved

First published 1984 by
André Deutsch Limited
105 Great Russell Street London WC1

ANDRE DEUTSCH

ISBN 0 233 97625 6
Printed in Great Britain by
Cambus Litho, East Kilbride, Scotland

Hector and Harriet's
Noisy Parties

Hector and Harriet were two naughty hamsters. They loved
escaping from their cage, and nearly every night they climbed
out and raided the larder or the vegetable garden.
They swung on the pea sticks, played catch with the peas,
and helped themselves to anything that took their fancy.

Then they'd run into the house to have noisy parties with the
mice under the floor boards, keeping Mr. and Mrs. Brown awake
all night. But Hector and Harriet always went back to their cage in
the early morning, so Mr. and Mrs. Brown always found them asleep.

"We must have mice," said
Mr. Brown one morning,
"I haven't slept for nights.
We'll have to get a dog to
keep them quiet."
So they did.

Bill the dog had big sharp teeth and a very fierce bark.
"Ah ha," said Mr. Brown, "now we'll have some peace."
But, what Mr. Brown didn't know was that hamsters
and cats terrified Bill.

That night Hector and Harriet escaped
as usual and danced into the larder . . .
straight into Bill!
"Wow wow wooow," howled Bill . . .

. . . and hid under the kitchen table.

"Ah ha," said Mr. Brown, listening in bed.

"Bill has stopped them." But, of course, Bill hadn't.

They raided the larder as planned and had a wonderful party with the mice, while Bill barked and howled above, making even more noise than usual.

"That stupid dog
will drive me crazy!"
cried Mr. Brown.
"We'll get a cat."
So they did.

Tom the cat looked very fierce with his big sharp claws.
"Ah ha," said Mr. Brown, "now we have a dog *and* a cat
we'll have some peace."
But . . . Mr. Brown didn't know that Tom was also terrified
of hamsters, and he hated dogs.

Mr. Brown left Tom the cat in the larder and
Bill the dog in the kitchen, then went to bed.
"Let's go and tease that dog,"
whispered Hector. So they
skipped to the larder singing,
"Isn't Bill a silly billy?"
But, instead of meeting Bill,
they danced straight into
Tom the CAT!

"HELP!" howled the cat and the hamsters.
"Wow wow wow," barked Bill, waking up,
and they all fled. Hector and Harriet raced
to their cage while the cat and the dog, rushing to
hide somewhere, collided under the kitchen table.

"Yeow pssssst!"
shrieked Tom.
"Wow wow wooow!"
howled Bill.

And first Tom chased
Bill all round the
house.

Then Bill chased
Tom all round the
garden, making so
much noise, the
whole village was
woken up.

Next day, Mr. Brown took Bill and Tom back to the pet shop, in disgrace.

That night, Hector and Harriet raided the larder and had
a wonderful party with the mice to celebrate the departure
of Bill and Tom . . . while Mr. Brown lay in bed upstairs.

"Isn't it lovely and quiet now that cat and dog have gone!"
he said to his wife, and they both rolled over and went to sleep.
The little squeaks and rustlings of the hamsters and the mice
didn't disturb them at all now, so the parties continued,
and Hector and Harriet had a lovely time every night.

Hector and Harriet
and the Little Empty House

One night, Hector and Harriet decided to explore the little
house next door. They ran across its garden, crawled under
the back door and began looking for the larder. But the
house was up for sale, and the rooms were dusty empty places with
nothing in them but cobwebs and dead flies.
"Oh it's horrid," whispered Harriet, "let's go home."
"In a minute," said Hector. "I just want to see what's in that room."

They went in, and found a large
object standing in a corner.
"I wonder what it is?" said Hector,
"come on, I'm climbing to the top."
"You'll never get up that," said Harriet
as she followed him.
"It's far too steep."

Half-way up Hector looked over the
side and noticed another large object.
"Oh," he said, "I wonder what that is?"
And, without any warning, he took a
flying leap . . . and landed on a piano!

"Derrrum!"

Hector jumped. "What was that?" he yelled.

"Derrrrum!"

It came again, resounding round the empty
house like thunder!
"Help!" cried Harriet, terrified. "Help!"
She leapt to the ground,
scampered across the room,
dived into the first hole she found,
and hid.

"It's a piano," laughed Hector, and ran up and down  "Tra la la la la la la,"
sang the piano every time he did so.
"Harriet, Harriet, come and join me, we could play a tune,"
he called. "Harriet, where are you?" he shouted, alarmed.
"I'm here," answered Harriet from her hiding place.

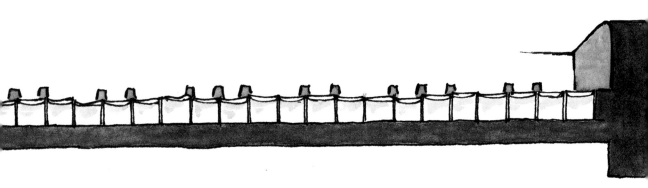

"Well, come up here," called Hector, as he danced on the keys.
After a while Harriet decided to join him. She tried to catch hold
of some wire stretched over the hole, and . . .

"Doing,"

it played loudly as she fell to the ground.
She was inside a broken old cello.

Harriet became·frantic.

"Hector, I'm trapped," she cried, desperately jumping up and trying to catch hold of the cello string.

🎵 "Doing doing doing,"

played the cello every time she did so.

🎵 "Doing doing doing."

But Hector didn't hear her.

"What a fantastic noise," he cried, dancing on the piano keys,

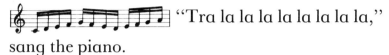 "Tra la la la la la la la la,"

sang the piano.

"Help! Help! Help!" screamed Harriet, jumping up and down

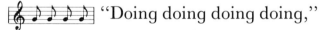 "Doing doing doing doing,"

called the cello. The little empty house shook with the noise!

Soon, all the people sleeping in the houses around were woken up.

"There's something going on in the
little empty house," they cried
with alarm. "Fetch the policeman."
The policeman was a nervous young man.
"I'm frightened," he said.
"Nonsense," said everyone. "Policemen
are never frightened." To feel
safer, as he was only in his pyjamas,
he put on his helmet, climbed a ladder
to a broken upstairs window,
and scrambled through.

"Oh d-dear," stuttered the policeman as he tip-toed gingerly across the creaking floor to the stairs, and went down.

"Doing doing, tra la tra la," sang the cello and piano.
"Oh g-goodness what a horrid dark noisy house,"
muttered the policeman, as he tried to pluck up
courage to enter the room with the music.

There was no one there.
Just an old mattress, a piano and a cello.
Who was playing the music?
The young policeman was so frightened, he ran upstairs and
scrambled out of the broken window as fast as he could.

"What is it? Who's there?" asked everyone.

"N-no one," stuttered the policeman. "N-no one at all.
Just a piano and a cello playing themselves . . . the house is empty!"

"EMPTY!" cried everyone. "Ghosts!" they shuddered. They ran
home, locked their doors and windows, and hid in their beds.

Presently, Hector became tired with his dancing and
sat down to rest.

"Help, help, help!" cried Harriet, still inside the cello,

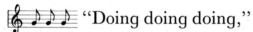 "Doing doing doing,"

sang the cello as she jumped wearily at the string.
Hector heard the cello for the first time. He rushed over
to it, peered into the hole and pulled Harriet out.

They ran home and went to bed. As they were going to
sleep, Harriet said, "Let's go again tomorrow night and
play a duet on the piano. I didn't like the cello at all."
After that, they often visited the little empty house
to dance and play tunes.
Sometimes they took their mice friends, too, and held parties.
What a time they had!

It was a long time before anyone had the courage to go into the little house again. When they did, and discovered it was only two hamsters and some mice who played the music, everyone said, "Well well well, just fancy!" A nice young couple with two children bought the house. Hector and Harriet still visited the house sometimes, and when they did the children woke to hear little tunes on the piano in the middle of the night.